NO LONGER PROPERTY OF
ANYTHINK LIBRARIES /
RANGEVIEW LIBRARY DISTRICT

 is for Yacht . . .

When Dink put his face underwater, he was amazed. The water was as clear as glass. Hundreds of fish darted every which way. He saw yellow, purple, blue, and red fish.

Ten feet below the surface lay the sunken boat. It was partly rotted away. Seaweed and barnacles clung to the boat's broken hull.

After about ten minutes of exploring, Hugo signaled that they should m____ ____ at his boat.

The kids padd____ ____ the side. They ren____ ____ mouthpieces so the____ ____.

"This is so amazing!" Josh said.

This is for John Gurney.
Thanks for your wonderful art!
—R.R.

To Molly
—J.S.G.

This is a work of fiction. Names, characters, places, and incidents either are the product of the author's imagination or are used fictitiously. Any resemblance to actual persons, living or dead, events, or locales is entirely coincidental.

Text copyright © 2005 by Ron Roy
Cover art copyright © 2015 by Stephen Gilpin
Interior illustrations copyright © 2005 by John Steven Gurney

All rights reserved. Published in the United States by Random House Children's Books, a division of Random House LLC, a Penguin Random House Company, New York. Originally published in paperback by Random House Children's Books, New York, in 2005.

Random House and the colophon and A to Z Mysteries are registered trademarks and A Stepping Stone Book and the colophon and the A to Z Mysteries colophon are trademarks of Random House LLC.

Visit us on the Web!
SteppingStonesBooks.com
randomhousekids.com

Educators and librarians, for a variety of teaching tools, visit us at RHTeachersLibrarians.com

Library of Congress Cataloging-in-Publication Data
Roy, Ron.
The yellow yacht / by Ron Roy ; illustrated by John Steven Gurney.
p. cm. — (A to Z mysteries)
"A Stepping Stone book."
Summary: Dink, Josh, and Ruth Rose help catch the thieves who have stolen gold from Sammi's parents, the king and queen of Costra.
ISBN 978-0-375-82482-1 (trade) — ISBN 978-0-375-92482-8 (lib. bdg.) —
ISBN 978-0-307-54990-7 (ebook)
[1. Mystery and detective stories. 2. Stealing—Fiction. 3. Kings, queens, rulers, etc.—Fiction.]
I. Gurney, John, ill. II. Title. III. Series: Roy, Ron. A to Z mysteries.
PZ7.R8139 Ye 2005 [Fic]—dc22 2004008066

Printed in the United States of America
27 26 25 24 23 22

This book has been officially leveled by using the F&P Text Level Gradient™ Leveling System.

Random House Children's Books supports the First Amendment and celebrates the right to read.

A to Z Mysteries®

The Yellow Yacht

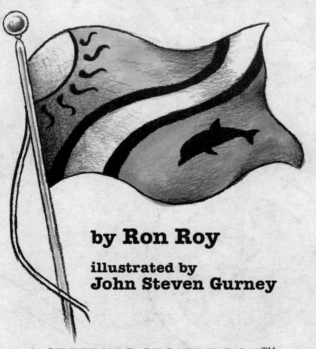

by **Ron Roy**

illustrated by
John Steven Gurney

A STEPPING STONE BOOK™

Random House 🏠 New York

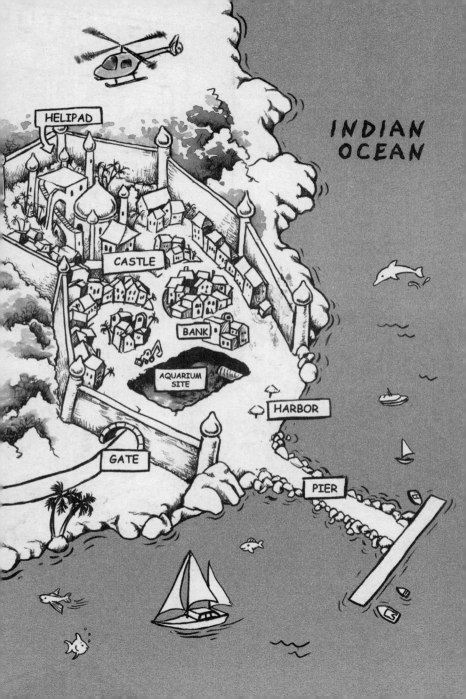

CHAPTER 1

"I'm going to miss you!" Dink's mother said as she pulled her car up to the airport. "Give Sammi a hug for me, will you?"

Dink's parents had named him Donald David Duncan, but now almost everyone called him Dink.

Dink, Josh, and Ruth Rose were on their way to visit their friend Samir Bin Oz for his birthday. Sammi lived in a small island country in the Indian Ocean called Costra, where his father and mother were the king and queen.

The kids hugged and said good-bye to Dink's mother. Then a man in a white shirt and dark trousers helped them stack their luggage on a cart.

"I'm Carl, your flight attendant on this trip," the man said. He guided the kids through security, then outside to the landing field. Off to one side sat a sleek jet. When the kids boarded, they discovered that they were the only passengers!

"Please choose your seats, then you can decide what you want for lunch," Carl said. He handed them menu cards.

"I love being treated like royalty!" Ruth Rose said. She liked to dress all in one color. For this trip to Costra, she had chosen royal blue.

While the kids were reading their menus, a redheaded woman stepped out of the cockpit.

"Hi, I'm Captain Rusty Dollar, your

pilot," she said. "Our flight to Costra should take about fifteen hours. When you wake up tomorrow morning, you'll be there. If you'll please buckle up, I'll take off in a few minutes!"

Five minutes later, the small jet roared into the air. The kids watched the ground become smaller and smaller. Then they saw only white clouds and blue sky.

When the plane had leveled off, Carl appeared at their seats. "What would you like for lunch?" he asked.

The kids all chose chocolate milk, cheeseburgers, and apple pie for dessert.

After they finished lunch, the kids played checkers, read, and listened to music through their headsets.

When it grew dark outside the small windows, Carl gave them each a blanket and pillow. He dimmed the cabin lights and turned on soft music.

"Pleasant dreams," Carl said, then he disappeared to the rear of the plane.

Dink woke up when he felt a slight bump. He sat up and looked out the window. He saw palm trees and blue skies. "We're here!" he said to Josh and Ruth Rose.

A few minutes later, the door opened and Sammi stepped inside the plane. He was wearing a ruby-red tunic and black pointed shoes.

"Sammi!" all three kids cried.

They all high-fived each other.

"Okay, you're free to deplane!" Captain Dollar said from the cockpit.

The kids thanked her and Carl, then walked off the plane to a small landing field. Warm air kissed their skin. A sweet smell came from flowers growing in nearby fields.

"Now where do we go?" Dink asked Sammi. "How do we get to your castle?"

Sammi grinned and pointed up at the sky. Just then the kids heard a whirring noise. A silver helicopter appeared above them. The rotating blades created a stiff wind, blowing the kids' hair every which way.

"We're going in a helicopter?" Josh cried. "This is the coolest thing that ever happened to me!"

The chopper landed, then the pilot helped the kids climb aboard and buckle up. As the chopper rose, it was too noisy to talk. Instead, the kids just watched the scenery down below.

Dink saw a deep blue ocean and boats of every size, shape, and color. Sunlight bounced off the water, turning everything to gold.

Five minutes later, the chopper started downward. Sammi poked Dink on the arm. "There's our house!" he shouted.

Dink, Josh, and Ruth Rose looked down at a small castle.

The chopper hovered for a few seconds, then landed on the castle roof. The pilot helped the kids climb out. He handed out their packs, waved, and took the chopper back up.

Dink squinted to keep dust and his hair out of his eyes. When he could see again, there was a tall man with bright blue eyes walking toward them. He wore a brilliant green robe with a yellow sash around his waist.

The man gave a slight bow to Dink, Josh, and Ruth Rose.

"I am King Farhad," he said in a deep voice.

CHAPTER 2

Dink gulped, then bowed to the king.

"And I am Queen Grace," said a woman who stepped out from behind the king.

The queen wore a long white gown. The tips of blue shoes showed under the gown's hem. Around her neck she wore a gold chain suspending a large ruby.

All three kids murmured "Hello" and bowed.

"These are my parents," Sammi said proudly.

"Welcome to our home," Queen Grace

said. "Sammi, why don't you show your friends their rooms now?"

The king and queen walked to a door, where a servant waited to open it. They disappeared down some stairs.

"This is so awesome," Josh said, gazing from the rooftop. The castle stood at the edge of a small town surrounded on three sides by an ancient wall. The fourth side was the ocean.

Beyond the wall were fields and woods. Dink saw a wide gate in the wall. A winding road snaked through the fields and disappeared into the mountains.

"Is that your father's boat?" Ruth Rose asked. She was pointing to a long yellow sailboat in the harbor. The yacht had a tall mast and neatly stowed sails.

"No, we only have a small fishing boat," Sammi said. He shielded his eyes and peered at the yacht. "I don't know who owns that one."

The kids followed Sammi down stone stairs to a carpeted hallway. A man stepped into their path. His eyes were fierce under thick black eyebrows. He wore a white turban, a black tunic, and red trousers.

The man smiled and nodded to Sammi. "May I help, young prince?"

"No, thanks, I'm just showing my friends their rooms," Sammi said. "Guys, this is Fin, my servant."

Fin glanced at the kids, then backed

away. "As you wish, young prince."

"He's scary!" Josh whispered.

Sammi grinned. "Fin is cool," he said. "He practices looking scary to keep kidnappers away. All the bedrooms are here." He pointed to a double set of doors at the end of the hall. "My parents sleep there, and our rooms are this way."

Sammi led them around a corner and stopped at the first door on the right. "This is my room. You guys can pick yours."

Dink counted eight closed doors. "These are all bedrooms?" he asked.

Sammi nodded. "Sometimes we have a lot of guests," he said.

Dink looked at Josh. "You want to share?" he asked.

"Sure. I know you're afraid of the dark," Josh teased. He opened the door of the room next to Sammi's and stepped inside.

"I'll take the one across the hall from you guys," Ruth Rose said.

"Okay, I'll see you in about ten minutes," Sammi said before he went into his room.

"Knock after you unpack," Ruth Rose told Dink. She went into her room and closed the door.

Before Dink had a chance to follow Josh, he heard a door open. A face peeked out of a room a few yards away. Dark eyes stared at Dink before the face disappeared and the door slammed shut.

Dink shrugged, wondering who else was staying in the castle.

Ten minutes later, Sammi led the kids into the town of Nere. They trekked along a cobblestone road under tall shade trees. Most of the old buildings were made of stone. Everybody they passed smiled and greeted Sammi.

At the harbor, they walked along a stone pier that led to a wide aluminum dock. The water was calm, and several boats and yachts were under sail or motor.

The yellow yacht seemed even bigger now that they were close. Dink noticed that it was not all yellow. There was a green stripe just above the waterline. The name *Sundown* was painted on the side.

"Maybe it belongs to a movie star!" Josh said.

As they gazed across the water, two

men in scuba-diving gear appeared on *Sundown*'s deck. They splashed over the side and disappeared.

"What're they doing?" Josh asked.

Sammi shrugged. "Maybe my dad knows," he said. "I'll ask him later."

Sammi led the kids farther along the harbor, then stopped where a huge, square hole had been carved out of the earth. Crisscrossing the bare earth was a maze of pipes and cables.

A row of boulders lined one wall of the hole. A green backhoe stood off to one side, like a sleeping dinosaur.

Two men stood together talking. One wore jeans and a T-shirt, with a red bandanna tied around his black hair. The other man was older with gray hair. He wore white pants and a blue shirt.

The man in the red bandanna waved at Sammi.

"That's Riko. He's the job foreman,"

Sammi said, with a wave back.

"What is this place, anyway?" Ruth Rose asked.

Sammi spread his arms. "It's going to be an aquarium!" he said. He pointed to the empty space behind the hole. "Up there will be a school for kids who want to learn about the ocean."

Sammi grinned at his guests. "Pretty soon, this will be filled with ocean water and plants and fish!" he said.

"What's that for?" Josh asked. He pointed to a long, wide pipe, half in the water and half out. A machine was attached to the end that was on dry land.

"A motor will pump ocean water up through that pipe," Sammi explained. "Other pipes will take the water out again, so it's always clean."

Dink pictured the finished aquarium with fish and other sea creatures swimming among those boulders.

Josh whistled. "And your dad is paying for all this!" he said.

Sammi pointed to a stone building next door. A small brass sign said NERE BANK.

"My grandfather left my father a lot of gold bars," Sammi said quietly. "They're in the bank, and that's what my father is using to pay for the aquarium."

"That's great," Dink said. "So when will the aquarium and school open?"

Sammi shrugged. "My dad says in a few months," he said. "Come on, I'll introduce you to Riko."

The kids followed Sammi down a sloping bank into the bottom of the pit.

Riko shook hands with all four kids. He greeted Sammi in Costran, a language Dink had never heard before.

"These are my American friends,

Dink, Josh, and Ruth Rose," Sammi said.

"Hello, and welcome," Riko said in perfect English. His eyes sparkled like black marbles and his teeth gleamed.

Riko turned to the gray-haired man. "This is Dr. Leopold Skor," he said. "He's giving me some great ideas for the project."

Dr. Skor bowed. "I am a marine biologist," he told the kids. "I am doing research nearby, and I heard about King Farhad's wonderful aquarium."

"Would you like to meet the king?" Sammi asked.

"You *know* him?" Dr. Skor asked, looking surprised.

"He's my father!" Sammi answered.

Suddenly they heard the sound of distant chimes.

"Come on!" Sammi said to his friends. "That's Fin ringing the dinner bell!"

CHAPTER 3

The kids spent the next couple of days exploring Nere.

Sammi showed the kids a small park where parrots lived in the trees. He took them to a glass-blowing factory, where they watched a man blow red molten glass into delicate animals. They stopped at a food stall and ate hot meat sandwiches and drank lemon-flavored drinks.

Once or twice, Dink noticed the man he'd seen peeking out of his bedroom in the castle. Dink asked Sammi about the

man, but Sammi just shrugged.

"He must be a friend of my father" was all Sammi would say.

On the third day of their visit, the kids were relaxing on a small beach. They sat in the sand and took off their sandals. The sun, puffy clouds, and boats made a beautiful picture.

Out in the harbor, the yellow yacht sat peacefully in the turquoise water. Every now and then, men wearing scuba gear would either jump off the

boat or climb aboard. They carried
mesh bags and wore long black flippers
on their feet.

The kids recognized Dr. Skor as he
walked about on the deck.

"Maybe they're looking at the fish,"
Josh suggested.

"Dr. Skor told my father he's studying coral," Sammi said. "But there's a lot
more coral outside the harbor," he said.

"His boat looks so cool. I wish
we could go aboard," Ruth Rose said

as she put her feet in the water.

"My father will arrange it," Sammi said.

Josh looked at him. "He can do that?"

Sammi grinned. "He *is* the king, Josh."

Just then Fin showed up with a few other servants, each carrying a large basket.

A few minutes later, they had set up a table and loaded it with food.

"Lunch is served!" Fin announced in Costran, and Sammi translated.

The kids loaded up plates and sat in folding chairs. The servants handed them cold drinks and cloth napkins.

"Oh my gosh, I just remembered!" Ruth Rose cried. "Today is your birthday, Sammi! Happy birthday!"

Sammi blushed. "My parents are giving me a party tonight," he said.

"Cool," Josh said. "Will there be a cake?"

Before Sammi could answer, they

heard a shrieking whistle. The noise was coming from town.

"What is that?" Dink asked Sammi.

"It's an alarm!" Sammi said. He stood up and looked toward town. "It sounds like it's coming from the aquarium site."

Fin leaned over and spoke urgently to Sammi in their language.

"Fin says he thinks it's the bank!" Sammi said. "Come on!"

The kids left their plates on their seats and raced toward the bank. Fin ran beside Sammi.

When they reached the bank, the door opened and a man burst outside.

"That's Mr. Lees Baz, the manager of the bank," Sammi said.

He ran over to Mr. Baz, who began speaking in rapid Costran. His eyes were bulging and he waved his hands in the air as he spoke.

Fin dug out a cell phone from inside his robe and dialed a number. People

came out of nearby shops to see what was the matter.

Sammi returned to the kids. His face was pale. "Mr. Baz said the bank vault has been broken into!"

"Did they take anything?" Ruth Rose asked.

Sammi gulped. "Yes, all my father's gold is gone!"

CHAPTER 4

Sammi said something to Mr. Baz, and the man nodded. He walked back into the bank, with Fin and the kids at his heels.

Mr. Baz took them to the vault. The door was wide open. Inside they could see a hole in the vault floor. Chunks of stone and concrete lay next to the opening.

Mr. Baz spoke excitedly to Sammi, then hurried away.

The kids peered down inside the hole. "There's a tunnel down there!"

Ruth Rose said. "The crooks dug their way in from outside somewhere."

Dink looked around the empty vault. The only thing he saw was a wide wooden platform. "Where was the gold kept?" he asked.

Sammi pointed to the pallet. "It was stacked there," he said glumly. "Fifty-two bars."

Dink knew that much gold would be very heavy. He wondered how anyone could carry it away.

Just then Sammi's father rushed into the bank vault, followed by a man and a woman wearing police uniforms. Mr. Baz stood beside them.

It was cool in the vault, but Dink noticed that Mr. Baz was sweating.

The king got on his knees to examine the hole, then stood up. "The tunnel was dug from the aquarium pit," he said. "Please check it, officers!"

The king turned to Mr. Baz. "Let's go

into your office, Lees," he said. "Fin, will you come, too, please? I'd like a witness to our conversation."

After the three men left, Sammi leaned close to Dink. "Let's follow the cops!" he whispered.

The four kids scooted out of the bank and walked to the edge of the construction site. Down in the pit, the officers were already talking to Riko and two other workers.

The kids moved closer so they could hear what was going on. They saw the policeman checking out the boulders lined up near the edge of the pit. He gave one of the boulders a tug.

"Hey, these things are fake!" he shouted in English. "They hardly weigh anything!"

To prove it, the man rolled the boulder out of line. It was as tall as him, but he moved it easily.

"They're all artificial," Riko said.

"They'll be used inside the aquarium when it's finished. Real boulders would be too heavy."

"Let's move them," the policewoman said.

Riko and his workers helped roll the boulders aside. It took only a few minutes to find the tunnel opening.

The policeman crawled into the tunnel while everyone else watched. He backed out two minutes later.

"There's food wrappers in the dirt," the officer reported. "I have a feeling someone spent a lot of time digging the tunnel."

The other officer looked at Riko. "Can you explain how anyone could have dug that tunnel without your knowledge?" she asked.

Riko shook his head.

"The tunnel was hidden behind the boulders. How was I supposed to know?" he asked.

"But you're in charge here, right, sir?" the policewoman asked.

"That's right," Riko said. "I'm the site foreman."

The officer beckoned to her partner to join her. "We need you gentlemen to come with us while we sort this out," she said.

One of the workmen started to pull away, but Riko stopped him. "Sure, we'll go with you," Riko said.

He led them to a sloping part of the pit, where the heavy machinery was driven in and out.

"Do you think Riko did it?" Ruth Rose asked Sammi when the officers and crew were gone.

"I hope not," Sammi said. "He seems like such a nice guy."

Josh peered inside the tunnel entrance. "It must have taken the crooks a while to dig this thing," he said.

"Let's check it out," Dink said.

The kids dropped to their knees and crawled into the tunnel. Dink went first, followed by Josh, then Ruth Rose. Sammi came last.

The tunnel was about the length of two school buses, but too low to allow standing up. The dirt under their knees was mostly sand and pebbles.

The kids could see with the help of dim light coming from both ends of the tunnel. They stopped in a spot that was wider than the rest of the passageway. Ten feet ahead, the tunnel sloped upward to the bank vault.

"Look at all this junk," Josh said. He pointed to a pile of burger wrappers and soda cans.

Dink kicked at the food debris. "I'd say he was in here a few days, at least."

"Wait, what's that?" Josh said. He scooted forward and grabbed a paper that Dink's sneaker had revealed.

"It's some kind of note," Dink said,

looking over Josh's shoulder. "But it's written in Costran, Sammi."

The kids hunched together while Sammi quickly read the note.

"This is impossible," Sammi said after a minute.

"What does it say?" Ruth Rose asked.

Sammi pointed to the words. "This was written to Riko," he explained. "It tells him to dump the gold over the wall, where someone else will load it into a truck and take it away."

The kids stared at the strange note.

"Is it signed?" Dink asked finally.

"No, but there's this." Sammi pointed to the bottom of the sheet. There, in small blue letters, was an e-mail address: LB@nerebank.net.

"This is the bank's e-mail address," Sammi said.

Dink put his finger on the first two letters. "These might be someone's initials," he said.

"They are," Sammi said. His dark eyes gleamed in the half-light. "LB stands for Lees Baz."

CHAPTER 5

"We have to show this note to your father!" Ruth Rose said.

"Yes," Sammi said. He took the note and slipped it into his pocket. "Pop's going to be really upset. Mr. Baz is one of his closest friends."

The kids crawled out of the tunnel.

They brushed dirt from their hands and knees, then stood looking at the backhoe.

"When do you think they stole the gold?" Dink asked the others.

"Probably over the weekend, when the bank was closed," Sammi said.

"But if they planned the theft together, why would Riko need to dig a tunnel?" Dink asked. "Mr. Baz could just open the vault and take the gold."

"Digging a tunnel into the vault would make it look like Mr. Baz wasn't involved," Ruth Rose said.

"But why would he use paper that had his own e-mail address at the bottom?" Dink went on.

"Maybe he meant to rip that part off and forgot," Sammi suggested.

"Maybe," Dink said. "But if I was robbing a bank, I'd destroy the note."

"How would they carry all that gold to the wall?" Ruth Rose asked.

"I'd use the backhoe," Josh said, heading toward the huge piece of equipment.

The scoop bucket was in the down position, resting on the ground. Josh stepped into the bucket and examined the metal edges.

"Take a look at this," he said. He had his finger on a shiny mark on the metal.

The others studied the mark.

"It looks like gold scrapings," Sammi said.

"You were right," Dink said. "They did use the backhoe to move the gold!"

Sammi pulled the note from his pocket and read it again. "This says Riko should bring the gold to the west wall, near the tree. Let's go check it out," he said.

The kids climbed out of the pit and headed for the west wall. They had to pass the castle in order to get to the gate.

"Shouldn't we tell your father about the note right away?" asked Dink.

"He's probably still in the bank," Sammi said. "Besides, this will only take a few minutes."

There was a tall tree near the west wall. The kids walked the ground beneath the tree, searching for clues. Ruth Rose had stepped a few yards away from the tree. She called the other three kids over. "Look, fat tire marks," she said.

The marks were only a few feet from the wall. Dink could easily picture what must have happened. The crook—was it Riko?—had driven the backhoe to this point, the bucket loaded with gold.

Then he had raised the backhoe's scoop and dumped the gold bars over the wall. Someone in a car or truck must have been waiting on the other side.

"Give me a boost, someone," Ruth Rose said. She had one arm wrapped around the tree as the other reached for the lowest branch.

"Where are you going?" Josh asked.

"If the crooks dumped a bunch of gold bars over this wall, there should be marks on the ground on the other side," Ruth Rose said. "Boost me up so I can see!"

The boys made footholds with their hands, and Ruth Rose scampered into the branches. Two minutes later, she was perched on the top of the wall.

"See anything?" Dink called up.

Ruth Rose looked down at the boys. "The bushes and weeds are all crushed," she said. "Like something very heavy dropped on them."

"Okay, I'm telling my father," Sammi said. "Come on down, Ruth Rose."

Ten minutes later, the four kids were sitting in the king's study. Sammi's father sat at his wooden desk, reading the note.

The king looked up. His normally cheerful eyes looked sad. "And you found this in the tunnel?" he asked.

"Yes," Josh said. "It was mixed in with some food wrappers and stuff. Whoever dug the tunnel must have dropped it."

"I just can't believe Riko and Lees would betray me like this," the king said sadly. "They both seemed eager to have the new aquarium open."

King Farhad sighed and reached for the phone. He called his police and told them to pick up Lees Baz immediately.

"Sammi, I'm sorry this had to happen on your special day," his father said as he hung up. "But I'll make it up to you later at your party."

Just then there was a light knock on the door.

"Come in," said the king.

"Your Highness," came a deep voice from the doorway.

The kids looked up. The man standing there wore a long black cape, and his head was completely bald.

Dink recognized the face he had seen peeking from a room upstairs a few days ago.

The man stepped forward and bowed in front of King Farhad. "Yondo at your service," he said.

The king nodded. "Kids, this is Yondo. He's a magician I've hired for Sammi's party tonight," he said.

"Cool!" Sammi said. "What kind of tricks do you do?" he asked the man.

Yondo wiggled his long fingers to show that his hands were empty. Then he reached over and pulled a large gold coin from the king's hair.

With a lightning-fast flick of his hand, Yondo flipped the coin at Dink. Dink raised his hands for the catch, but it never reached him.

The coin had disappeared into thin air.

CHAPTER 6

The four kids entered the royal dining room at seven o'clock. The table was set with a white tablecloth that reached the floor. The queen's best dishes sparkled under the candlelight.

The king and queen smiled at the kids. "This is your night, Sammi. There will be no discussion of the missing gold," the king stated.

In the middle of the table sat three large pizzas.

"How did you know pizza is my favorite meal?" Josh asked, rubbing his stomach.

Sammi grinned. "It's *my* favorite, too!" he said.

A half hour later, only pizza crusts were left. A servant cleared the table.

"Time to open your presents," Sammi's mother said. Stacked on a nearby table were the gifts Dink, Josh, and Ruth Rose had brought in their luggage.

Dink's present was a book about Connecticut. He showed Sammi a map inside and pointed out Green Lawn.

Josh gave Sammi a small wooden eagle. "I carved it myself," Josh said, blushing.

"It's awesome," Sammi said. "Thanks, Josh!"

Ruth Rose brought a travel-size Monopoly game. "I thought we could play after dinner," she said. "But watch out for Josh. He cheats!"

The king set a large, gold-foiled box

in front of Sammi. "This is from your
mother and me," he said. "Happy birthday, son."

Sammi tore off the paper to find a
new computer. He gave his mother and
father hugs. "Thank you, it's just what I
wanted!"

"Now we can e-mail each other!"
Ruth Rose said.

"Excellent," said the king. "And now, Yondo is going to entertain us."

The king clapped his hands and the room lights dimmed. A door opened and everyone watched for the magician to enter. But there was no one there.

"Yondo at your service," came a voice from the opposite side of the room. When they turned, Yondo stood at the end of the table, next to the queen. He was dressed entirely in white.

"How did you get in here?" Sammi said. "There's only one door!"

Instead of answering, Yondo pulled a green bandanna out of Sammi's ear.

For the next twenty minutes, Yondo amazed them with magic tricks, doing one right after the other.

He tied knots in colored hankies and let the kids check that the knots were tight. Then he ran his hand over the knots, and the hankies separated.

He turned normal eggs into rabbits

and rabbits into beautiful doves.

He wet two fingers and snuffed out a candle. Then he opened his mouth and breathed fire like a dragon.

"For my final illusion, I will make one of you disappear," Yondo said to the small group. Then he pulled a large black cloth from a sleeve and shook it out, covering himself. When the cloth dropped, Yondo was gone. In his place stood a tall silver box about the size of an old-fashioned phone booth.

A door in the box opened, and Yondo stepped out. But now he was dressed from head to toe in red.

Yondo smiled at Ruth Rose. "Will you be my assistant?" he asked.

"Okay, but be sure to bring me back again," Ruth Rose said.

Yondo led Ruth Rose into the box. He closed the door and draped the black cloth over it. Then he knocked on the cloth with his knuckle. "Are you still in there, Ruth Rose?" he asked.

"No, I'm up here!" came Ruth Rose's voice from above their heads.

Everyone looked up toward the ceiling. It was dark, so the king turned up the lights.

Ruth Rose was nowhere in sight.

Yondo knocked on the box again.

"Ruth Rose, are you in there?"

This time there was no answer.

Josh let out a giggle. "She really *did* disappear!" he whispered.

Yondo whisked the cloth away from the box and opened the door.

It was empty. The three boys leaped up and examined the box.

"What're you all looking at?" Ruth Rose asked from behind them.

The boys whipped around. Ruth Rose was back in her seat at the table.

"How did you do that?" Josh asked Ruth Rose.

"I'll never tell," she said.

Just then a servant carried in a cake with ten lit candles on it.

Yondo started to leave.

"Please stay for some cake," the king said with a smile. "As long as you don't make it disappear!"

Yondo smiled. "Only my piece will disappear," he said.

Sammi made a wish and blew out the candles, and they ate.

"I'm gonna bust open," Josh said later as the servant cleared the table.

King Farhad and Queen Grace excused themselves. "You kids can sit up and play Monopoly if you wish," the queen said. "But not too late, Sammi."

The kids decided to play in Sammi's room. As they climbed the stairs toward the bedroom wing, Dink was thinking about the missing gold. "Sammi, where did your father find Yondo?" he asked.

"I don't know," Sammi said. "I was just as surprised to see him as you guys."

"Does he live in Costra, or did he fly here, like we did?" Dink asked.

"Why? Does it matter?" asked Sammi.

"I'm not sure," Dink said. "But don't you think it's strange that your father's gold disappeared right after Yondo got here?"

CHAPTER 7

"What, you think Yondo stole the gold?" Sammi asked.

"Well, he made a lot of *other* stuff disappear," Dink said. "Like you, Ruth Rose."

"He didn't make me disappear," Ruth Rose said. "It was a trick. While you guys were changing for the party, Yondo asked me to help him. See, he's a ventriloquist, too. He threw my voice up to the ceiling. When you guys all looked up there, I scooted out of the box and crawled under the table. Then I just got up and sat back in my chair again."

"If Yondo is the thief, where did he hide the gold?" Sammi asked Dink. "And how would he get it away from Nere? The guards check every car going through the gate. No one could get past them."

"Except maybe a magician," Dink mumbled.

"I think Riko and Mr. Baz are the crooks," Ruth Rose said.

"I hate to admit it, but I agree with Ruth Rose," Josh said. "I think Mr. Baz was on the other side of the wall with the getaway car, waiting for Riko to drop the gold over."

"They both told the cops they had never seen that note," Sammi said. "Mr. Baz said someone must have stolen that writing paper from his office."

Just then a shadow fell over the kids. Yondo had appeared at the top of the stairs.

"We meet again," the magician said. "What are you whispering about?"

"We're just talking about the gold robbery," Sammi said.

"Ah, yes, your parents told me about the bank manager and the job foreman," Yondo said. "What a shame. Well, I leave early tomorrow morning, so I will say good night. And happy birthday, Sammi."

Yondo walked past the kids and disappeared into his room. They all heard the door lock.

The next morning, the kids walked down to the aquarium pit. No one was working in it. Yellow crime-scene tape had been strung around the whole place. The backhoe stood right where it had been left.

The bank was locked up, with a big CLOSED sign on the door.

"I wonder if my father will ever get

the gold back," Sammi said.

"Did Yondo leave yet?" Dink asked.

Sammi nodded. "I saw him drive away this morning," he said.

"Hello!" the kids heard someone yell from behind them.

Dr. Skor had tied a yellow inflatable dinghy to the dock and was walking toward them.

"Any news on the robbery?" he asked when he reached the four kids.

Sammi brought him up to date on Riko and Mr. Baz.

Dr. Skor nodded. "Yes, I assumed it was an inside job," he said. "At least the culprits are behind bars, where they belong. And how was your party, Sammi?"

"Cool! My dad hired a magician, and he was awesome!" Sammi said.

"A magician, how wonderful!"

Dr. Skor showed the kids a grocery

shopping list. "I must get to the store. Your parents are joining me for lunch on my boat," he said. "You kids are invited, too, of course!" He hurried off toward the shops.

"I hope Dr. Skor is a good cook!" Josh said.

At noon, a sturdy-looking fiberglass boat pulled up to the dock. A boy who looked about sixteen years old was at the motor. He wore a bathing suit and a tank top.

"Hi, Hugo!" Sammi cried. "These are my friends Dink, Josh, and Ruth Rose. They're from Connecticut in America."

"I want to visit your country some-day," Hugo said. "Do you live near New York City?"

"Yes," Dink said. "My uncle Warren lives there. If you come to visit, you can stay with us!"

Hugo beamed. "Thank you!"

"Hugo is going to study at the new

school," the king told the kids. "And one day he'll work at the aquarium."

Hugo helped everyone aboard and motored toward the yellow yacht.

"How are you spending your summer vacation?" the queen asked Hugo.

The boy grinned. "I'm doing a lot of diving and snorkeling," he said.

"Do you see a lot of fish around here?" asked Josh.

Hugo nodded. "Every size and color you can imagine," he said. "I'll take you guys snorkeling later if you want."

Sammi looked at his parents. "Can we?" he asked.

His father said, "Of course. Hugo, do you have four life vests?"

"Yes, sir," Hugo said. He looked at his diver's watch. "How about three o'clock?"

"Excellent!" Sammi said. "I've got snorkel gear you guys can borrow."

A few minutes later, Hugo dropped

them off, and they climbed aboard *Sundown.*

"Please come back for us at two o'clock!" the king called back to Hugo.

Hugo saluted. "I'll be here," he said.

Soon the lunch guests were seated on comfortable benches around a table on *Sundown's* foredeck. A canvas canopy kept the sun off.

"Your boat is beautiful!" Ruth Rose told Dr. Skor.

"Thank you, my dear," Dr. Skor said. "Would you like to explore her before we eat?"

"Sure!" she said.

The kids scampered away. They examined every part of the yacht, fore and aft. In the galley, they found a stove, sink, and refrigerator. A man was preparing their lunches.

There were three bedrooms. The kids stepped inside the largest onto a bright blue carpet. The room had a king-size bed and a chair near an open porthole.

Next to the door was an antique desk. Dink saw papers and letters with Dr. Skor's name on them. Holding down a few letters was a paperweight in the shape of a small boat. Dink saw a green stripe on the boat and realized it was a miniature replica of *Sundown*.

Just then they heard a bell ring above them.

"Lunch!" Josh said, and the kids headed for the stairs.

CHAPTER 8

"Dr. Skor, my husband told me you're studying coral, is that right?" the queen asked as the lunch dishes were being cleared.

"Yes," Dr. Skor said. "Coral is dying and . . . wait, I have some photographs."

Dr. Skor left the table and returned with a photo album.

They flipped through the pages as Dr. Skor showed them pictures of healthy coral and sick or dead coral.

"When coral dies, other sea life dies," the scientist said.

"Is this a picture of *Sundown*?" Ruth Rose asked him, pointing at another photograph.

"Yes, I took this with my Polaroid camera when we arrived here a few days ago," Dr. Skor said. "Isn't she beautiful?"

This snapshot showed *Sundown* with her sails up, puffed from a breeze. The yellow paint gleamed above the green stripe. In the background, Dink could see the stone pier and the castle.

"Do you fish off the boat?" Josh asked.

"I don't, but my men do," Dr. Skor said.

"Do you like to fish, Josh?" the king asked.

"Yes, sir, I love it," Josh answered.

"Then maybe we can do some fishing before you leave," the king said.

"This has been lovely," the queen told

Dr. Skor. "Please come have dinner with us soon. Your food was delicious, but now I need a nap!"

Dr. Skor smiled. "This is my nap time, too," he said. "And I'm afraid I can't accept your kind invitation. We sail this afternoon, as soon as the breeze picks up."

"I'm sorry you're leaving," the king said, "but thank you for your suggestions on my project. Do come back and see us when the aquarium is up and running."

There was a pause, as if everyone was wondering if the aquarium would ever get finished.

They said good-bye, and minutes later, Hugo's flat-bottomed boat pulled up. They all climbed aboard and headed back to the dock.

Dink turned around and looked over Hugo's shoulder at *Sundown*. He could see Dr. Skor standing on the foredeck, watching them through binoculars.

Watching the yacht get farther away, Dink didn't see the green stripe. He rubbed his eyes. How could the stripe just disappear? he wondered.

While the queen napped and the king talked with the police, Sammi outfitted the kids with snorkel equipment.

At three o'clock, they were waiting on the dock for Hugo.

Hugo showed up a few minutes later. His boat left a small wake as it bumped gently up against the dock. "Climb in!" he said.

"Will we see any sharks?" Josh asked as the kids clambered down into the boat.

"Not where we're going." Hugo pointed to the right, just outside the harbor entrance. "See that red buoy sticking up? It's marking the place where a boat sank a long time ago," he said. "The water is shallow and lots of fish hang out there. Perfect for snorkeling!"

Hugo handed the four kids orange life vests and made sure they were fitted properly. He aimed the boat out into the harbor, and a few minutes later, he reached the buoy. He stopped the engine and dropped the anchor. Then he tossed a float with a small flag attached to it into the water.

"This flag lets other boaters know there are people in the water here," Hugo explained. "When they see the flag, they stay away."

Hugo helped the kids with their snorkels, masks, and flippers. He jumped into the water and showed them how to clamp the snorkel's mouthpiece in their teeth and breathe.

When the kids were floating in the water, Hugo and Sammi showed them how to swim facedown, using just their flippers and no arms.

"If you need me, just tap the top of your head with your hand like this," Hugo said, demonstrating. "If I see that signal, I'll swim right over."

With Hugo leading, the four kids flippered a few yards away from the flag.

When Dink put his face underwater, he was amazed. The water was as clear as glass. Hundreds of fish darted every which way. He saw yellow, purple, blue, and red fish.

Ten feet below the surface lay the sunken boat. It was partly rotted away. Seaweed and barnacles clung to the boat's broken hull. Several large rocks sat on the boat's bottom.

The kids stayed near each other. Hugo pointed to a creature that looked like a lobster, but it didn't have big claws.

When the creature saw the humans, it darted under the boat.

After about ten minutes of exploring,

Hugo signaled that they should meet him at his boat.

The kids paddled over and held on to the side. They removed their masks and mouthpieces so they could talk.

"This is so amazing!" Josh said. "A purple fish came right up to my mask and looked at me!"

"Hugo, why are there rocks in the sunken boat?" Dink asked.

"The rocks are to weigh it down so it won't drift away," Hugo said. "The boat attracts fish."

Suddenly Dink knew why *Sundown*'s green stripe was missing. He felt his heart start to race. Goose bumps marched up his arms.

"Guys, I think I know where the gold is," Dink said.

CHAPTER 9

Hugo helped the kids climb back aboard his boat. They sat drying in the sun while Dink explained to them what he suspected.

"I think Dr. Skor stole the gold," he said. "And I think it's on his boat."

"But where?" asked Ruth Rose. "Remember, he let us look around. Wouldn't he be afraid we'd find the gold by accident?"

"And what about Yondo and Riko and Mr. Baz?" Sammi asked.

"Yeah, and the note we found about

dropping the gold over the wall," Josh added.

Dink shook his head, and water drops flew from his hair. "I think Dr. Skor put that note in the tunnel, where the cops could find it," he said. "I'll bet he had his crew dig the tunnel. He wanted the cops to think Riko and Mr. Baz pulled off the robbery."

"But what about the gold scraping we saw on the backhoe shovel?" Sammi asked.

"That was another of Dr. Skor's fake clues," Dink said. "The cops would search for the gold on land, but the gold is really on his boat."

Hugo gazed across the water at *Sundown*. "Why do you think it's on his boat, Dink?"

"The first time we saw *Sundown*, there was a green stripe above the waterline," Dink said. He pointed across the harbor at *Sundown*. "But look, there's no green stripe now. It came to me when I saw the rocks weighing down the sunken boat. The gold is making *Sundown* heavier! The green stripe is still there, only we can't see it now because it's underwater!"

Five pairs of eyes stared across the harbor at *Sundown*.

"Where could it be hidden?" Ruth Rose asked.

"If I stole that gold, I'd stash it under the boat," Hugo said. "If the cops searched *Sundown*, they'd never think of

looking on the bottom of the boat."

Hugo switched on the boat's engine. "Haul up the anchor, Sammi," he said. "Let's check out the *Sundown*."

Hugo motored slowly toward the yellow yacht. "Try not to look suspicious," he said quietly. "Pretend we're just cruising around the harbor."

Hugo pulled up to *Sundown*'s anchor chain and tied up next to Dr. Skor's small dinghy. He slowed the engine so the motor was barely making a sound.

"We're behind the boat, so unless someone's on the rear deck, they can't see us," Hugo whispered.

Dink squinted up at the deck. "I don't see anyone," he said. "Dr. Skor told us he takes naps in the afternoon."

"Okay," Hugo said, reaching for his mask. "I'm going in. If anyone says anything, just tell them I'm checking something on my motor."

Hugo donned his mask and flippers

and slipped over the side. He took a deep breath and disappeared beneath the water.

The four kids stared at the spot where Hugo went under. They saw him disappear in the shadowy water under *Sundown*.

They counted the seconds, holding their breath for Hugo.

Suddenly a voice came from the rear deck of *Sundown*. "What're you doing down there? You can't tie up on our anchor line!"

The kids looked up. They saw the man who had been making their lunches in *Sundown*'s galley.

Dink gulped. Before he could form an answer, Hugo's face broke the surface. He blew out the breath he'd been holding, then hoisted himself into his boat.

"Is that your boat?" the man on the deck shouted down.

"Yes, sir," Hugo shouted back. "Had a little trouble with my propeller, but it's okay now."

Hugo untied his line and pulled away. He turned toward the dock and revved up.

"Did you see anything?" Dink asked. He was trembling all over, and it wasn't from the boat's vibrations.

"Oh yeah," Hugo said with a big grin on his face. "I saw plenty!"

"Did you find my father's gold?" Sammi asked.

"Yes, it's there," he said. "Skor built a steel cage between the keel and the propeller. The gold is stacked in the cage."

The kids all looked back at *Sundown*.

"He told us he's leaving port today," Ruth Rose said.

"He can't sail because there's no wind," Hugo said. "Which means he has to use his motor. The good news is his motor is small. He can't go very fast."

CHAPTER 10

Hugo dropped the kids off on the dock. "Run and get your father," he said. "I'm going back out there to keep an eye on *Sundown!*"

With Sammi in the lead, the kids raced for the castle. The king was on the telephone in his office when they burst in.

The king looked up. "Sammi, I'm talking to the police. Can you pl—"

"We found the gold!" Sammi blurted out.

The king's mouth dropped open.

"Where?" he asked, ignoring the telephone.

"Dink figured it out," Sammi told his father. "Dr. Skor hid the gold underneath his boat!"

Interrupting each other, the kids quickly explained how Hugo had swum beneath the yacht and spotted the gold.

"But you have to hurry, Pop," Sammi said. "A guy on *Sundown* saw us. He'll tell Dr. Skor, and they'll take off!"

The king spoke into the telephone. "Surround that yellow yacht in the harbor!" he ordered. "And have your fastest boat pick me up at the dock in three minutes!"

The kids were surprised at how fast the king could run. He made it to the dock before they did and leaped into a sleek police boat. The boat practically flew out of the water as it sped toward *Sundown*.

Hugo zoomed back to the dock and whistled. The kids climbed into his boat, and he raced after the police.

By now three police boats had tied up to *Sundown*. As Hugo and the kids approached, Dink could see several officers boarding the yacht.

"Look!" Ruth Rose suddenly yelled. She pointed aft, where Dr. Skor sat in his rubber dinghy.

The man started the motor and the dinghy roared toward open sea.

"He's getting away!" Ruth Rose yelled.

"Can you catch him?" Dink asked.

Hugo grinned. "Do fish drink water?" he asked. "Hold on!"

Hugo thrust the throttle all the way forward. His boat tore around *Sundown* with its bow out of the water.

The kids grabbed their seats and braced themselves as they bounced over the water.

Ruth Rose was sitting next to Hugo. "You steer!" he yelled in her ear. "Use both hands and get as close as you can to his dinghy!"

Dink, Josh, and Sammi stared as Ruth
Rose and Hugo switched places. Her
knuckles were white as she clutched the
steering wheel.

Hugo picked up the anchor. It had

three sharp prongs that were meant to grab and hold. A long rope was tied to the anchor. The rope's other end was attached to a metal ring on the bow.

"Can you get any closer?" Hugo shouted to Ruth Rose.

"Do monkeys eat bananas?" she shouted back. She turned the wheel, and the boat responded.

When his boat was about fifteen feet from the dinghy, Hugo stood up. He spread his legs for balance, then whipped the anchor over his head.

The steel anchor landed in Dr. Skor's rubber dinghy with a thud. Hugo grabbed the wheel from Ruth Rose and whipped it around. Then he shoved the throttle forward, and his boat lurched ahead.

Dink didn't understand what Hugo was up to. Was he planning to tow Dr. Skor's dinghy back to shore?

But then he got it. The anchor rope stretched to the breaking point, but it held. Suddenly they all heard a ripping noise. The anchor hooks had torn a hole in Dr. Skor's dinghy. When they looked, it was losing air fast.

Dr. Skor turned and glared at Hugo and his passengers. The thief's face was nearly purple with rage.

Just then two police boats roared up to them. "Good job, kids," one of the officers said. "We'll take it from here."

Riko and Mr. Baz were released from jail. Dr. Skor and his crew took their place. Police divers brought the gold ashore, and it was once more locked in the bank vault.

Riko's crew repaired the vault floor

and filled in the tunnel. The yellow crime-scene tape came down, and work began on the aquarium again.

"And I have you kids to thank for saving the day," the king said. Sammi had invited Hugo to join them for ice cream and leftover birthday cake.

"If Dink hadn't noticed the green stripe was gone, Dr. Skor would have gotten away with it," Ruth Rose said.

"How did you figure it out?" the queen asked Dink.

"At first, I thought Yondo took the gold," Dink admitted. "But when we were exploring Dr. Skor's boat, we saw a paperweight on his desk."

"A *paperweight* gave you a clue?" Josh said.

"Not then," Dink said. "I just remembered that it was a miniature copy of *Sundown*, even with the green stripe. Later, when we were snorkeling, Hugo told us the sunken boat had rocks in it to weigh it down. Then I remembered a strange thing about Dr. Skor's boat. I couldn't see the green stripe and wondered why. The next thing that popped into my head was, something heavy must be weighing the yacht down. Something made the stripe sink below the water."

"And of course it was gold," the king said. He raised his lemonade glass to Dink. "Excellent reasoning, young man."

"How did Dr. Skor get the gold to his boat?" Josh asked.

"He told the cops his men took it out through the aquarium pipe," the king said. "They just slid the gold bars right into the water, probably at night. Then his crew moved the gold underwater to that platform he'd already built onto *Sundown*'s bottom."

"But how could the men swim while carrying that heavy gold?" Ruth Rose asked.

The king looked at Hugo. "Why don't you tell them?" he said.

"Everything weighs less in the water," Hugo explained. "The crooks probably wore scuba equipment. They could easily carry the gold in baskets like deep-sea divers use."

The king grinned at Dink, Josh, and Ruth Rose. "I don't know how to thank you," he said.

"I do," Josh announced. He reached for the last piece of Sammi's birthday cake.

HAVE YOU READ ALL THE BOOKS IN THE

A to Z Mysteries®

SERIES?

Help Dink, Josh, and Ruth Rose . . .

. . . solve mysteries from A to Z!

Collect clues with
Dink, Josh, and Ruth Rose
in their next exciting
adventure!

THE
ZOMBIE
ZONE

The moonlight touched the fence and the gravestones. The two empty graves were black holes with mounds of dirt piled next to them.

"I guess I was wrong," Dink whispered. "I thought for sure—"

Suddenly Josh slapped his hand over Dink's mouth. Then Dink heard Ruth Rose gasp.

One of the empty graves was glowing! As the kids watched, two hands emerged, grabbing at the edge of the hole.

Excerpt copyright © 2005 by Ron Roy. Published by Random House Children's Books, a division of Random House LLC, a Penguin Random House Company, New York.

A TO Z MYSTERIES® fans, check out Ron Roy's other great mystery series!

Capital Mysteries

#1: Who Cloned the President?
#2: Kidnapped at the Capital
#3: The Skeleton in the Smithsonian
#4: A Spy in the White House
#5: Who Broke Lincoln's Thumb?
#6: Fireworks at the FBI
#7: Trouble at the Treasury
#8: Mystery at the Washington Monument
#9: A Thief at the National Zoo
#10: The Election-Day Disaster
#11: The Secret at Jefferson's Mansion
#12: The Ghost at Camp David
#13: Trapped on the D.C. Train!
#14: Turkey Trouble on the National Mall

Calendar Mysteries

January Joker
February Friend
March Mischief
April Adventure
May Magic
June Jam
July Jitters
August Acrobat
September Sneakers
October Ogre
November Night
December Dog
New Year's Eve Thieves

If you like **A TO Z MYSTERIES**®,
take a swing at

#1: The Fenway Foul-Up

#2: The Pinstripe Ghost

#3: The L.A. Dodger

#4: The Astro Outlaw

#5: The All-Star Joker

#6: The Wrigley Riddle

#7: The San Francisco Splash

#8: The Missing Marlin

#9: The Philly Fake

#10: The Rookie Blue Jay

#11: The Tiger Troubles

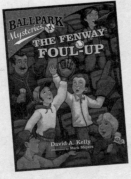

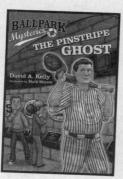